DON'T BUY
THIS BOOK
IF YOU ARE
STUPID,
BECAUSE IT'S
PROBABLY
ABOUT
YOU

DON'T BUY THIS BOOK IF YOU ARE STUPID, BECAUSE IT'S PROBABLY ABOUT YOU

EDWARD J. RYDZY

DON'T BUY THIS BOOK IF YOU ARE STUPID, BECAUSE IT'S PROBABLY ABOUT YOU

iUniverse books may be ordered through booksellers or by contacting:

iUniverse
1663 Liberty Drive
Bloomington, IN 47403
www.iuniverse.com
1-800-Authors (1-800-288-4677)

Because of the dynamic nature of the Internet, any web addresses or links contained in this book may have changed since publication and may no longer be valid. The views expressed in this work are solely those of the author and do not necessarily reflect the views of the publisher, and the publisher hereby disclaims any responsibility for them.

Any people depicted in stock imagery provided by Thinkstock are models, and such images are being used for illustrative purposes only. Certain stock imagery © Thinkstock.

ISBN: 978-1-5320-1185-6 (sc)
ISBN: 978-1-5320-1487-1 (e)

Library of Congress Control Number: 2016921371

Print information available on the last page.

iUniverse rev. date: 01/14/2017

Don't buy this book if you're stupid,
it's probably about you!

There is a rage and limit to everyone's virtue.
There is a limit to everyone's pain and perseverance.
The is not a limit to cruelty or the
horrors that you will see.
Nor is there a limit to the stupidity
that can be found out there.

I suggest that you ride the "life train" as long as you can.
Because no one is certain of what is next....
with that said...

Let's get to this Book.

THIS BOOK IS FOR MATURE AUDIANCES ONLY.

No one under 18 should even skim through this book, ever!

Don't buy this book if you are stupid...
… it's probably about you !

By
(the all seeing)

Edward J. Rydzy

Before the big mean "naughty words" scare you off:
THINK !

We have a government that says they are trying to help save you from yourselves or whatever...

Then WHY... do they allow smoking and drinking but get really put out by you not wearing a seat belt? AND, to add morally bankrupt philosophy to that... you have "people" that do these drugs, smoking and drinking, but will toss away an entire meal if "dog forbid" it hits the table or someone accidentally touches the edges with their fingers. IDIOTS!

They want you to prosper, but they will gang rape you if you do not pay your taxes. They will audit you or I for an extra $100 a week, but large corps get billion dollar tax breaks. Idiots!

Did every imbecile read this cover? Good.

Here are some more prerequisites for reading this book also. If you do not fit these put the damn book down and walk your simple ass away.

I am not here to impress you with my (non) Ivy League College large words and superior spell and grammar check.

I am not here to tell you my degree is in Psychiatry, paranormal or "popular" crap or whatever.

I am not here to show you a layout of pretty pictures

I am not here to have you all agree with me... this here is not "job one"!

If you do not like curse words, Fuck Off

If you do not like words like fag-got, nigger and other crap like this, Fuck Off

If you love any god a lot, tell the asshole to pray for me to die or stop writing books or ...Fuck Off.

As you can tell, Religion is not my favorite topic, but it's funny and something that I can easily pick on and deal with.

If your ego is so damn fragile that words will destroy you, well you should know what comes next right?

<u>Basically here is my real resume:</u>

I am 52 and way smarter than you

Ex. Military, but not Rambo

College, but no Masters

World traveler, but not the whole world

Father but only a few kids, not 5 – 10

Business man, but far from rich

Hate politics; stop voting, you're just encouraging them

Not religious, I read the book, it sucked and contradicted itself the entire time.

Here is the NON-righteous part of the book:

I am NOT perfect in any way. I am the THINKING creature and I will never stop being one, for any amount of money, threats or treats. I just love expressing my "THOUGHT OUT" feelings and knowledge. I write the way I LIKE it, not the way we are "supposed to write". My book here is from My Heart and experiences. If you do not like it, no hard feelings, go buy another book, that is grammatically right, spell checked perfect and done by a ghoul with a giant degree and a small personality. No problems.

Now, for you few (probably very few) intrepid warriors who are continuing reading this, let's see how many of us agree or at least understand and respect my (the) views on the world.

So you like DEAD ON, STRAIGHT Honesty do you... hmmm... we'll see !

There is a person that used to own this store before me and he won't publish his book, because the towns people will use pitch forks and torches to chase him out. Yes they are out there.

In one episode of STAR TREK, the Original series. The crew met Abraham Lincoln. He said to Uhura, "CHARMING NEGRESS...Before he could apologize, Uhura said, "in this century we have learned not to Fear Words..." Will we ever make it this far?

I don't share that fear !
I don't share much of anything, except my views!
I ask for nothing in return, but... I hope I am remembered!

If not at least give us a real talk show host. An unscripted and brutally honest one. The closest thing we have to that is that pseudo fag Tosh.0

I am not sure of the author here, but here goes:
>You tell on yourself by the things you wear
>By the way in which you part your hair.
>By the books you choose from a well filled shelf
>In these ways and more, *you tell on yourself!*

If at all possible I want you to remember this little tid bit. It is the Iching of this book. Not the grammar or the typos... it's the inner meaning that we have all forgot or now CHOOSE to accept or reject.

No matter what you think of this book, it's from the heart and the truth as I have seen it, from the 60's to now! Deal with it!

CONTENTS

1. Driving in America 1
2. Religion and the Bible 7
3. Restaurants and Mini-Markets 14
4. Real Family Life 19
5. Alternate Life Styles 24
6. Cops: Friends Or Foes 28
7. Lawyers, Not the Tv Lawyers, the Real Ones 35
8. Government: Friend or Foe 38
9. Surviving Teen Years: Bullying 41
10. Surviving Adult Hood 45
11. Television Kinda... Sucks! 48
12. Computer Age: Never Leaving It 53
13. Why the Amish are So Cool, or Not? 56
14. Social Media: You Need it, You're Still Dumb 60
15. Jobs Damn it, Jobs! 62
16. China Fucking Sucks, Deal With It! 64
17. Yes Pot, Weed or Marijuana is a Drug, Idiots! 68
18. Stupid Movies Of All Times 70
19. If you could read minds...? 72
20. My Alien Friend And I Have Had Some Great
    Conversations 75
21. The Supernatural Versus Reality 82

22. Shit sucking college and school students from hell. . 86
23. Women 89
24. Racial Retardation 91
25. The Friends I've Known 94

CHAPTER 1

DRIVING IN AMERICA

Starting with this lovely topic we have to dissect the two sides to everything:

- Old vs. Young
- Inner City vs. Rural
- SMART vs. FUCKING STUPID...

...The last one is the one that matters.

Now I don't mean *book smart*, I mean common sense wise

To quote ARISTOTLE: Well begun is half done. So let's start this book off right.

Most of you are not at fault for driving like old crack heads. Most of you were taught by old fashioned people that actually had to pay for their mistakes, not scream: I have a lawyer, it's because I am black, or I am suing the car company, its a recall problem.

I am sincerely ashamed of people that do not pay attention or respect the fact that they are driving around in over 2 tons of metal. It's about time you fools kept the flow of traffic going and stay alert and aware of your environment... god damn morons!

Here is what makes me write about drivers:

1. If you drive under 55 on the highway, you're a fuck head, keep it flowing assholes

2. If you pull out in front of me and go slow or turn immediately, you suck shit!

3. If you are on your cell phone and swerving all over, fucking die ...please!

4. If you are old and feel that 15 mph in the city works, fuck off. I believe the old farts of the world should have to take a *dexterity drivers test* after 65 to keep their licenses also. Yes, you're a danger, jerk offs. What possible defense do you have?

5. If you think you can take up two (or more) parking places because you're an inbred redneck with a F250 or whatever, you're as shitty as what you shovel and drive and *you deserve your life.*

6. If you like to throw you cigarette butts out the window...join them on the way out and make room for respectful, non-littering persons on the road, you fucking cocks. Stop sleeping with your cousins, Idiots!

7. If you think I'm fast, good. You're slow, and I don't want to stay behind you, so stop whining and drive

8. If you get mad at me for passing you, drive faster Grammy, I have a life. Places to go, things to do

9. If your kids drive better than you & their balls haven't dropped yet, you suck!

10. If you think I am wrong. That's okay... You Still Suck, learn how to drive !

11. If your face is almost smashed up against the windshield and you are white knuckling the fucking steering wheel, *get off the road assholes*!

12. Basically; if you are insecure, afraid of every car that passes you, or you do not really want to drive... then don't drive! Save my friends & Family's lives

13. On second thought, forget it. Stay off the road ass. I'll feel much better.

14. I really love these school speed limits too. I mean do we really need to crawl around schools? "Oh, but you're saving my kids, don't you love your kids, you monster"? Yeah, my two pack a day smoking teenagers that never listen to teachers and demand to be treated like adults... screw em! I mean in my days, a teacher could smack a brat. Maybe we should bring it back? Maybe?

15. BLINKERS! Fucking USE THEM !!!!

16. Now do not forget: the government wants to protect you from traffic, so they enforce seat belt laws... but NOW they are legalizing pot, repealed prohibition and never thought twice about cigarettes, but they're looking out for your safety. Idiots. But whose worst, them for making more money for them to spend on them (wow! Lots of *them,* hunh?

17. You know... as I constantly drive around in this same area, I came to the extremely harsh realization that I am not normal, I am a mutant and no one finds me funny, because ... well here is my list of stupidity and accepted abnormalities:

    ✓ These people (like most of you) are not in any type of hurry... I AM

    ✓ These people do not work. Most of them are on disability...I AM NOT

- ✓ These people save their money for needs: like cigarettes, beer and drugs...I DO NOT
- ✓ These people are afraid to drive near the speed limit as they are wasted...I AM NOT
- ✓ These people are not licensed, due to losing their licenses to DWI...I HAVE MINE
- ✓ Most people have no road courtesies, they care about no one but themselves, until church or *family get together's*. And with their gene pool getting real shallow, this also accounts for their driving terrors. That and the fact they've been in more accidents then most of their NASCAR heroes... I have been in 0 accidents, 37 years.

I know so many prime examples of road stupidity, I just do not know where to begin... Yeah, I do.

- I got this gal pal whom cannot drive at night or near the yellow line. I explain to her she's a nervous driver. She says no, she just doesn't like driving near other cars or yellow lines. So if you don't like crowds you have agoraphobia or are just a fucking coward? Choose Dick.
- I know this guy who thinks he is the toughest fuck around, but he cannot drive in or near a city (25K or more). What?
- I know a gal that stopped right in the middle of an intersection because her friend said look. She looked and another car, she obviously did not see, ran over the top of their hood and she almost died. She didn't get it.

Remember now: this is the ONLY thing that the <u>police</u> can do right in regards to enforcing the law. They can't help beaten women, business owners reporting losses, etc. Just Traffic.

Finally: I know this person that every day takes up 2 parking places. She *retardedly* gets offended if you nicely ask her to try to park right. This is the world in a nut shell. Basically: a fool learns nothing from a wise man, a wise man learns much from a fool.

I would say I am surrounded by fools, but I would be insulting fools everywhere...and even congress deserves the benefit of the doubt (fuck no they don't... baboons).

If ten people tell you that you have a tail... FUCKING LOOK !

AGAIN: the problem with drivers is that they are NOT smart enough or courteous enough to know that there are OTHER people on the road besides them.

If they know there are other people and they don't change their ways, they are cock suckers. If they don't know there are other people then they are a Danger to themselves and others.

BASICALLY: Treat everyone like they're stupid. You'll have a high percentage of Being Right !

But above all, PLEASE...

PROTECT YOURSELF.

MAKE CITIZEN ARRESTS

The police do not care. They're over worked,
underpaid and greatly disrespected.
They can do nothing, but quote laws.

IT IS BETTER TO BE JUDGED BY 12...
THAN CARRIED BY 6...

Chapter 2

Religion and the Bible

Oh my god where do I start with this one.

In truth, I really do not want to beat this puppy too much. I know there is no god and that does not bother me, because I know we need a myth to make us all feel better... and most of the real evil people I know would be even worst if they did not think that there is an easy way to a mythic heaven...i.e; "Hey, god. I am sorry, can I still go up there instead of that real hot place". "Yes, I know I killed, raped and murdered, but... can I please go up there"? "I'll be reborn", "Oh, yeah. I can. Gee thanks. I was hoping that loop hole still applied. I was worried I might have actually got what I really deserved".

Here is what makes me write about the bible:

1. Not inspired by any god, or chapters would never have been left out, doy! If you are so afraid of a god put in all the information. Do not omit shit that the almighty told you to write or inspired you, like the elders of yesteryear did. Fact.

2. A god that does not appear is the same as a non-existent god, jerks! PROVE IT, you say. Could you say that in a court of law? This is the only topic that people feel does not need to be proven in a court of law, save the scopes monkey trial. haha

3. If you want to know about incest, mass murder, etc. Read the whole book. None of you have, I know this because you would not believe in it if you did. It's way to stupid, contradictory and a lie.

4. If you get your wisdom from this goofy tome, watch Hollywood, it's better!

5. If you believe Atheist should get their own government, because America is a christian based nation, then you are a fool...keep reading the bible. And yet, as screwy as America is, maybe you're correct. We Butcher and neglect people too.

6. If you believe the bible proves god is real, then I have some spider-man comics and webs all over new york city, that prove spider-man is real also!

7. Hey, it's much easier to read only ONE book for all your education and beliefs. Hell yeah. Math, Social Sciences, etc. Suck. Read the Bible, cling to it tight, and skip over the horrible stuff like, closing up woman's wombs, nuking people with fireballs ...and especially, murdering everyone by drowning them. Slow death is the coolest. Don't turn them to salt, or lightning bolt them, or... you know any quick deaths. Torture the fuckers gasping for air, while their babies die right next to them as they are unable to save them, etc. Yep kill all *dem* fuckers!

8. Love the *in god we trust* thing on those dollars. I really don't mind them, that is what god is all about right? He (who did not need to eat, etc.) had to have his food sacrifices from Cane and Abel. Hey, I know what its like to miss a meal, it sucks. But we send our kids to bed hungry if they do something wrong, don't we? Or we used to.
9. Keep tithing also. Small businesses need to go out, while churches grow!

Here are some real winners in the christian world:

- Pat Robertson
- Jim Jones
- Adolf Hitler

I mean this list is endless too but you see where I am going with this, yes? Religion does not make better people, nothing does. There are no such things as perfect people, just perfect intensions.

What I am saying in a nutshell here, for all you nuts is:

There is no ONE answer. There are thousands of religions in this world with thousands of origins, but YOU have the exact perfect true one. Look there is only ONE you. Think for yourself or put your life is others' hands.

I know there are many whom never had a choice in this matter. Most of them do NOT want to discuss this, because they KNOW that their book has mistakes. That does not make it invalid, it just means there is much room for many unanswerable questions.

Ancient Aliens
Other Pagan or Earthly gods
Dimensional Beings or Ghosts.

Who the hell knows? If any of these exist
then your god of mythology does not.
He said he chased off all the fake gods.

Take care of each other, because the only world you are
guaranteed is this one!

So fucking cliche I could barely put that to type, here
is something better:

*we are what we repeatedly do. Excellence
is not an act, but a habit.*
Thank you Aristotle
no gods, ghosts, goblins, ghouls or giants
here... just us *wee* humans.
But it's always fun to watch these Christians
and the like smoke, drink, do drugs, etc.
Strong faith here, or just convenience, fear and
the need to fit in. Either way, it's a party.
Basically, grow up and take responsibility for your own life
and problems, morons! Or, there is the horoscope. haha

Did you know this land of freedom was formed ONLY
by people whom had a vision or had talked to this christian
god to begin with. There was nothing free about this new
world. Self governing hypocrites founded this country and
still do control it.

Some more fun personal facts here:

- I remember growing up, this kid told me he wanted
  to join the priesthood. The next day I saw him and
  2 other boys holding this boy up and "*punking*"
  him real bad.
- Priests and young boys... do I need to say more

- if you have used this phrase, "it's god's will or it's god's reasons alone". Keep tithing. It means you actually have no thoughts of your own, and you deserve what you are going to get
- oh and... god watches you masturbate ... and, so do I. (not really, but it makes the book funnier.
- Why do you cry when your friends and family die? They're going to heaven, right? No? Stop crying and buy some more religious junk.
- Have any you EVER really read the entire book, front to back? If you did, you'd cry.

I started this blog one time that basically said the bible is a joke and I can prove it. This was the longest running blog ever, until some 13 year old wanted to beat me and said, "lets just post anything here to make Ed's blog not the longest".

I was not angry because I learned so much from this and this is: People are afraid of death, going against tradition, and being alone.

These people kept going back to "well how did the world begin"?

Ask Neil D. Tyson to answer this paranoia that you keep as you cling to out dated, unintelligent words from a book that constantly contradicts themselves. Please don't ask me to quote these constant contradictions, just look them up, they are all over the internet. And when you do find them, don't stop believing, you most likely need some heroes in your life, there are none left in the real world... or...are there?

1. Firemen
2. Policemen
3. Military People

4. Your Parents
5. Your community that you love, you love them for a reason
6. Your family
7. Your favorite comic book, the good guy still wins here
8. Your best friend, he/she is your BFF for a reason, yes?
9. Your school/college teachers
10. Lastly: YOURSELF !

Do you really fear death so much that you'd blindly give your money and faith to this little establishment?

I am also afraid of death, but as they said in the *Last Samuri*, "will you tell me how he died"? The response was, "No, I will tell you how he lived".

People, I am so fucking happy you can believe in the unproven, but give him all this credit when something goes right in your life.

I am so happy that you sacrifice so much for a far fetched maybe at best, etc...

I am sure there is an afterlife, but how much of your REAL life are you willing to give up for this chance of an:

*   unproven book
*   unproven god
*   a god whose myth is only the work of other mythes
*   a god whom made great mistakes, like making man in his image, down plays women importance, hates gays-they're an abomination, circumcision, etc...

Don't pray for what you can do yourself. Just do it! Work those three jobs. Stay with that crazy wife. Stick that nutty job out

Be the best you can be, do just accept your place in the world.

At the end I will list MANY contradictions of the bible. Whether you like it or not !

CHAPTER 3

RESTAURANTS AND MINI-MARKETS

Now why do you go from religion to restaurants? Because they are both equally important. And restaurant workers are finally getting real money. Yay!

And I like eating way more than praying to any mythic being... with that said:

Do you know what really pisses me off? (Not yet you don't. But you will ...).

People that frequent these places show how stupid and ignorant they really are. I have at least 100 examples here, but I will try to break them down into more fun and interesting items:

Here are some of my personal experiences in stores and restaurants:

1. One guy came into the store. The prices were raised 20 cents on the beer. He said, "How do you expect me to eat with the prices constantly going up"? Funny Drunk.

2. One gal, we give extra small items too for free, seen our price of milk. She was immediately offended and said that she would rather travel 6 miles than pay this price. Loyalty? Nope.

3. One dude, wacked out on drugs, stole something. When my wife asked him where is the deodorant, he said it's back on the shelf, next to the kool-aid? (Weird). He went back there and pulled it out of his pocket and walked it back to my wife. To this day he sells and buys drugs in the park across the street constantly threatening in sue us for slander. Idiots are not born, they are made, by bad parents and drugs. He is par for the course around here.

4. Speaking of bad parents. In my town and many others, it is not rare to see 6 – 9 year old just running around, being sent to the store, with no shoes or shirts (in NY, this law has been in effect since the 70's), stealing and begging for candy and food. Masterful indeed sirs. Idiots!

5. One person in a restaurant came in an complained about their fries. Over half eaten they wanted a new one. The manager on shift said, Okay, but they are almost gone. The customer said that the manager was rude. I think the customer was stupid.

6. Now, on the flip side. A bunch of teens (about 4) came into the store and said, "Hey, we just skateboarded about 4 miles, can we get a fountain soda please? We will split it". I was so in awe of how tactful and classy the kids were, I gave them a small one each, for free.

7. One older bitch stood in line asking for lottery ticket after lottery ticket, etc. This went on for about

20 minutes. The man behind them finally handed me a 20 and said pump 3 please. I took it and rang him up. The old crone said, "well that was rude". I laughed, she left. It was a better day.

8. In my store you better believe about 50% of the people are potheads. One pothead got mad at me because I asked my nephew to keep this kid away from my daughter. He thought I wasn't being a good role model. I almost said, "so pot is what you want your kids to do"... I was at least trying to protect my daughter. Can't wait for him to have kids. In fact I sincerely hope that ALL kids of parents that are druggies start smoking and drinking at the earliest age possible. Super Curse for these righteous dumb fuckers, hunh? Yep, I thought so also. Let's see these idiots defend drugs once it hits them right in their own home. Just admit your a weak or pray to get rid of it. Jeez!

9. The usual here is, the parents buy their beer and cigarettes, and then complain that the kids want a dollar or less piece of candy.

10. Finally, this one lady misread the kerosine pump. It said, 7 gallons. She thought it was 7 dollars. She ran out screaming, "You made the mistake, I get the gas for free". Yes, I got the license and reported her. Her husband came in and paid with an apology. I guess she thought we were Wal-mart or something. Remember, these people do not think they're dumb. Luckily for them, I *know* they are.

11. A regular customer came into our store and said, "hey, can I get a loan"? I told him, sorry, but we do

not do that anymore. He said to me he will take his business elsewhere. I said, what business and with what money? He later apologized.

12. Another customer came in with no shirt or no shoes... do I have to say anymore? No, I think not... and neither did he I guess. Drugs are a horrible thing...lack of literacy also sucks.

13. Another customer works in one of our local places with kids. She sells drugs and takes them. Again, Any thing else needed here?

14. Now, I have people like this coming into my store all the time. The population in this area is about 1400 and steadily declining... here is why, let me continue. One gal owns a small shop in the area and she has: lied about cashing a check in my store, lied to the local Amish and did not pay for her roof getting done, because they won't sue, and we watched her buy tons of seafood at a place on her ebt or snap card. There is more, but...

15. one time two imbecilic older ladies were really arguing about Gore and G.W. I pulled out a jello and watched them. They looked at me and asked me what I thought. I said the Jello is great and on sale. One left, one paid for her gas then left.

16. One time I was able to stop 15 black people from entering the E.R. At a capital city hospital by simply saying, "who is the injured one?" they answered, I continued, "Let's get her medical attention and you all get seats in the waiting room." A glorious day you'd think. A few ours later 3 white people, 2 guys and a gal. Came in for "I don't know". They picked

fights and had to be removed. The one gal wanted to fight our female agent. It was a hoot...assholes!

17. You can tell the people that have NEVER ran a business. Running a business and managing one are totally different things. I see totally different things slithering into my life every day. I have learned some tolerance, but I still love being me.

The mark of a great educated mind is to hear and accept a thought into your head, and be able to not accept it fully, unless you really want to. Education is equal to mental strength.

Small businesses are constantly harangued by the government. Large businesses get *uber* tax breaks, etc. Small businesses get audited for claiming they pay too much for electricity. 100 dollars vs. 100 Million tax breaks. I don't get it?

It's tough to be a real person these days, isn't it?

Are you?

This one friend of mine asked the group, "I wonder if these girls are just nice to us for tips"? We all of course laughed and said, no Mike, they ALL just like you a lot.

Working in a restaurant or convenience store can make you go either of two ways: your own, or theirs.

It, like life, is being able to sort out what is what is people wanting you to join them in their insanity. I'm my own monkey. PERIOD!

Chapter 4

Real Family Life

Let's start with the "how many people believe that their family is normal"? ....LIARS!

It is normal... to you! But what is normal. Here are some interesting people that I know.

1. Do you think that a parent that spanks is evil or a lazy parent? No. I don't, but do you?
2. Do you think that a parent has the right to home school? Yes. I do.
3. Do you ... etc.

We can do this all day and all night, but in truth there is NO real book on parenting...

As I watch the "Parents" of the town I am in, I say to myself, "Are you fucking kidding me"?

Now, I do not say this *just* about my hometown here, as I have lived all over the world. I say this with the knowledge of many states, cities and a few countries. Here are some of my experiences:

1. One local parent loves to tell his now 19 year old son that he should not do POT because it's bad. Now this guy is a pot head, smokes and drinks and his son knows it... now I want all of you two faced people to say this immortal creed with me, *"Don't do as I do, do as I say"*! Who loves or has loved, to have heard this from their parent(s)? Yes...everyone.

2. My roof my rules, but... what if their rules suck? My daughter thinks my rules suck. No tattoo's, no cutting, no smoking, no drugs, no sex, no piercings, no talking back, etc. I'm a monster.

3. I know a woman that was totally abused as a kid, but thinks the world of her parents. You have to accept nothing, deal with it.

4. I have watched a kid fall to the ground and throw a fit, because they could not get candy, kick their fucking ass, until they hate candy or you! My mom used to say, "if you hate me I did my job right".

5. one kid went into a parts store with his parent working there. Something toppled over on him as he climbed on it, unsupervised by the parent. The kid's parent sued the store. Assholes! Kill all the Lawyers, right Billy?

6. I watch many country folks let their kids adventure at 2 – 4 years old, and still wonder why many farm accidents happen to them.

7. I also have witnessed inner city kids running totally wild, while their oblivious parents (or so you think) just keep on shopping and ignoring what is happening. But these parents will be the first to sue or cry for hours and days, if something were to happen to their angels.

8. If you are one of those LAZY parents that just give in and;
   - buy their kids anything.
   - Let their kids monopolize their time in stores
   - let the kids talk back to adults
   - do not discipline their kids at all because they are either in fear of the government or what other stupid fucking parents might think: you DESERVE your horrible future with these horrible spoiled ne'er-do-wells you are sprouting. Live with it. You suck at parenting and I hope your kids shoot you for not buying them a blow-pop one day...at 15! Then you can say, I just don't understand, I followed Dr. Phil to the letter.

NOW, to slam dunk this irony here, let's talk **Marriage.** Do you know how many men just cringed in disgust? Most. Why?

Of course it is harder for men in many ways to get married, but mostly because:
   - we lose everything upon divorce and
   - we cheat or they cheat and we lose everything.

Now this is not to say that women do not cheat also, that would be a stupid fucking statement, but... when women cheat, they still get the kids. Men get the bills.

Again this is NOT an ironclad statement and many times women can lose the children also, pending on drug use, infidelity, income and other things, but in my days, if a woman could dress and feed the kid, she got em.

I want to say it's a brave new world, but it's not. Women still want doors held open, man buys dinner, etc, but damn it, is respect in there somewhere, ha?

Now for all you nurturing, wannabe mothers out there, here is my suggestions, FUCKING listen / read with me here:

1. If you need a Prenuptial agreement, don't fucking get married you goddamn bimbo
2. If you are the only one working, don't get fucking married you goddamn bimbo
3. If you don't want to introduce him to your family, don't get married you fucking bimbo
4. If you get *HIT* in any way before you get serious, like moving in, etc. Don't get married you fucking bimbo. He showed you the real him, believe me!
5. If sex sucks, he does drugs, drinks in excess, etc. What kind of a stupid attitude is this? I Don't get it
6. Do not get married because men marry women hoping they don't change, stupid fucking women marry men, hoping they do! Surprise Bimbos.
7. There is a fun statement that claims that the only way to avoid PAIN is to have NO desires. This is the most true statement ever. This applies to every aspect of life, but I (and most of you) cannot and SHOULD not lack desires. Desires are so cool and they keep us going and interested in life itself. So unless you are planning on joining the Monks of *neverland*, you better get used to disappointments.

Here is a "WTF" moment: my wife has had two back operations. She has to travel over 45 minutes to get to a pain management place that sends her home half the time, because the doctor calls of because he's sick. The doctors won't even consider giving her disability, because they do not want to get involved in the lengthy court time proving it, but... over 40% of the area is on disability. They drink, smoke and do drugs like they don't care. My wife and I hold down two small businesses that make NO money at all. When I see all these dregs of society, skulking around here drugging up and my wife not sleeping more than 2 hours at a time, because of pain. I wonder why I do what I do.

Something interesting happened to me when they told me my father died.

They said, "He dies peacefully".

What a bunch of shit!

What are they going to tell you?

1.   He died screaming and shouting
2.   He died as blood oozed out of his eyes
3.   He died cursing your name
4.   He died crawling on the floor to get meds
5.   He died like a 4 year old girl, crying, etc...

The punchline to this joke is, like in any good X-files show, *The Truth Is Out There.*

Do we want to hear the truth 100% of the time?

SHIT NO!

But there are times when i'd rather get it on the Chin, then in the Back.

Chapter 5

Alternate Life Styles

I have been waiting to get to this one for days, it seems.

Okay, let's see, what can I say about gays? Oh my dog, way too much.

Starting with, here you have a life style that is so *off the trodden path,* that you can not even see where weird starts and happiness ends.

Most of these queer little beings are so happy to immediately announce how gay they are you don't even get a chance to judge them, but, they do so worry about it.

"Don't judge me, I was born this way".
BULL SHIT ! ! ! !

You were born like all of us, certain types of abuse, neglect of other social problems led you to *BECOME* what you are or think you are, today. You were raped, beaten by a Jewish dad, failed out of baseball, etc. I don't know, but I am SURE that before you took a penis up your ass there was something that menaced you, in some way. If not (and you are sure) than I would advise you to look hard into your soul, before you go down Greenwich village parading your faith in this gay-way.

We're here and we're queer... who fucking cares!

Here is what pisses me off about this fucking movement: (and I can only imagine the types of movements you have)

1. You have to tell everyone? Hey guys, I just nailed my wife yesterday...sounds weird? How about: Hey guys, I just had a threesome...

2. ***Let's start having **SCHOOLS** teach alternate life style sexuality. Sure, we can tell them the wonders of having your ASS stretched to the Nth degree in the hopes of finding love. Or licking that carpet or pounding it with a fake 'wee wee' or... who knows, maybe we need more young fags? Why not? Lets see how open your minds really are? Hmmmm?***

3. Then they can have fun going to the adoption agency and asking for a child that they can "rear" and show the way too. "*We will take the ones that are born gay only please*". Idiots! '*Did Lady Gaga Birth any of these ones*"?

4. The real Irony is that if the world were full of faggots, then the guys would rule. Women would NEED them to procreate the species and make more 'Hershey Highway' traveling ghouls. Do you understand this. Women would be almost forgotten

5. Maybe Obama and the white house brigade could put up more rainbows on the front lawn to support this miraculous and proud culture in America.

6. Or at birth, with this "Gay Gene", we can start using segregation in schools again. I think this would

give an entire different definition to the Humanities programs. Haha. Morons!

7. Or maybe we can SEPARATE this gay gene and only make the type of gays we want. Maybe we can make bestiality kids and then... werewolves! And in New Jersey, toxic tikes. Oh yeah!

What I am saying ass-bites is that, and *fucking listen to me*, *THIS DEVIANT LIFE STYLE SHOULD NOT BE WHAT IS DEFINING YOU*!

You are just too fucking stupid to know or recognize it. You are too happy to be an "Out cast" or something different, You do not realize that it is not impressive or getting you any type of respectable attention;

It's like arguing about your myth of choice. Whether it's Christianity, Jewish, or whatever... it's just your idiotic opinion. And I promise you, NO ONE FUCKING CARES !

1. I just want to be left alone, like the Mormons, whom go door to door, but close theirs (in Utah) from anyone ever seeing them.

2. Oh, but we will get discriminated against and looked down upon. DOY! You started it. Not Biology or a spiritual blessing or curse, ... you!

3. My one pal gets mad when I use the word faggot, but is not mad at all that Police get slammed for any type of problem that they do not cause or are not part of.

4. *You have to be stronger than your pains.* If not the fucking world will eat you up, spit you out and ONLY REMEMBER the bad that you have done!

5. I don't understand the reason why people are so afraid to say it like it is: You have the RIGHT to NOT like homosexuality, just like these fops have to right to be queer.

6. You have the right to turn yourself into a minority and yell at the world, but as I said earlier, NO … you were NOT born that way… Idiots! Deal with your CHOICE and accept the consequences. If you want to leave the norm of society, then…enjoy! The world is not perfect. Your decision, while making you happy are not perfect. Just like hecklers and bullies, they are wrong, but if unchecked, they're just plain evil. But like rappers, they're here to stay

CHAPTER 6

COPS: FRIENDS OR FOES

Another interesting, and kept out of conversations topic. "Well, I don't want to be a negative nitwit, but cops are bad". Who the fuck starts off conversations like this. It's like saying, "I don't want to be negative but all blacks are bad" or "All non- Christians are evil"... get it?

Most police do not go into the law because they want to be corrupt. Like most politicians, most (I think) want to help people. Do nurses become nurses so they can bang and marry doctors? I sincerely do not think so. The *rules* of thumb for any business:

1. If you do not ask for trouble, very rarely will you get it, or...if you do get it, IT won't be as mercilessly and and horribly enforced.

2. If you drive like an ass (like me) you will most likely get a ticket, IF you have many tickets already, you will keep collecting them.

3. If you have priors, you will turn yourself into a pulp comic book series that no one wants to buy.

4. "Oh, but look at Ferguson or the O.J. Trial or..." Hey, *Fucktards*, building a shrine to an imbecile is like making posters of Charles Manson and trying to sell them. Good luck in bankruptcy court.

5. KARMA-You'll not escape it in this life or the next

6. Don't blame the cops for being an ass: The crime is not that you got caught, it's the crime itself.

7. Do cops make mistakes? Sure. Do we? Sure. Does every business or occupation in America make mistakes? Doctors, Accountants, etc. Sure.

8. When you make a mistake, say, "Oops, I stepped on my dick and drive on". Life's to short. You either get BITTER or BETTER, that is it. One fucking letter. I have been at rock bottom, but I drove on. I did not quit. I exhausted my resources. I survived. I am a pretty impressive creature. Are you?

In the movie "Billy Jack" (old 60's movie), he says, "when the police men break the law, there is no law. Only a fight for survival".

I like to feel that most of the time, most of the police officers do not (intentionally) break the law, just enforce it.

I like to feel that most of the Doctors cure people.

I like to feel most of the politicians...er... fuck this one!

Now as for my personal experiences: I find them all law quoting lackeys. We don't need police any more, just lawyers that get there and say, "no we can't arrest them for slapping around this woman, because we did not see it. But she should leave him". AND how does she do that? Most of her family has no money. The police refuse to help or protect her. She can put a restraining order on him, but when he breaks down the door and beats her stupid, she'll lift it and the poundings commence!

The sad fact of the world is that the police are not evil, they are worthless. They can give traffic tickets and break up a bar fight and that is it.

Sorry. I just say it like it is.

It's a shame that we have to have guns that we don't dare use, like the police.

It's a shame we whom follow the laws get them used against us.

It's a shame that usually the ones whom get bullies by the police are the meek and semi innocent. They do this because they are afraid of the real criminals.

It's a shame.

My suggestions to you are: Write a book, get rich and live off the grid. But a gun, and 4 dogs and only go into town for supplies. I plan on this, so everyone, please buy the fucking book.

The only respect the police have is the traffic laws. Again, it's a shame that they can not dole out justice like Judge Dredd. Would this make a better world?

Would it make a worse world?

Would it make a safe world?

All I know is that it is going to be a horrible world my kids will grow up in, and I cannot protect them.

I cry often

I do.

The UBER funny thing here is there is no REAL C.S.I. Here or any where near it. CSI is an unreal television show that is found NO WHERE in America.

I could kill, rob, and destroy half the area before I was even suspected.

Why you say? (Glad you asked).

Because they all hire their cousins.

These people are really not at fault, we do not usually have any great emergencies or problems here.

A guilty as hell woman will get off for killing her abusive boyfriend or husband, because there is sympathy for her... and there should be, but...

A person... well let me point this out to you:

We own a half a million a year business, fueled by food stamps and pennies scrimped together by out local faithfuls...

Would you like to see my expenses? Yes, I know you do.

1.	Electicity:	$2500 a month (on a good month)
2.	Rent	$400
3.	Morgage	$500
4.	Pay back investor	$1000
5.	Cars	$1300
6.	Grocery order	$9000
7.	Insurances	$1000
8.	Salaries	$2000
9.	Misc. Vendors	$4000
10.	Garbage	$50
11.	Misc. Payments:items	$200
12.	Misc. repairs/upkeep	$500
13.	cable, telephone, etc.	$500

Right now I am hoovering at $17000 a month, TIMES 12= 250k sounds like a deal hunh? Now take out 30% profit that you make: that puts you at: 150k to pay all this stuff with...

That's puts us at a NEGATIVE (-) 75k

This was documented in our income tax and this was with me just knuckle-balling the numbers (pretty close hunh?)

I put this under the police category because they actually audited us a while ago. If it was not for our great accountant and our keeping close track of these numbers WE (my wife and I) would have went to jail.

This is what our government finds important.

NOW, on the flip side, I mentioned earlier, we are Super SURROUNED by drug addicts and drug dealers. They all live here because we are on the edge of two counties, where the Sheriffs can't help and there are no uniformed police near us, so... the SCUM sneak into this area and make a well protected home.

Now, If I was to go out at night and deal with these SCUM who do you think would get in trouble?

Yep, tell me when you caught up? This is why I have to write this book.

In about 2 years my family and I will be homeless. I would digress to being a cat burglar, but I am old and fat, can't do that. I can not work more than 2 jobs (old and fat, remember), my credit is declining also because I can't keep up with stuff and all the people in the area think we're rich businessmen, so they patronize use when they can or when they find it convenient (hence the name 'convenience store').

But again, my kids will be 18 in a few years (YAY) and they can find a nice studio apartment and huddle around burning newspapers (my other business that makes nothing, and I have almost 700 papers there), with us providing outdated items from our dormant store... but, if I shop lift a crescent roll, I will do time, as these drug pukes keep on, keeping on.

I am not unique. New York State hates small business. They will give all sorts of tax breaks to the rich, but unless you read EVERY fine print benefit, that they MIGHT offer us small business persons, they will simply take and take from you. The police can keep their jobs and offer nothing but traffic details to the area, but we few...we happy few...we band of broke brothers, will have to soldier on somewhere else. Hey, thanx for listening to this rant. If you can't afford the book, send your non-perishables to my store and family... we will fucking need them very soon.

Love you all...not really, but poverty sucks. We've taught in China, managed businesses and been totally poor and almost homeless...our egos are involved here, just the desire to take care of our family in this unforgiving area in central/ upstate NY.

A friend of mine insisted that I add this to my book. The police (in Troy) have a New "bedside – or curbside- manner".

Upon being pulled over my friend was asked for his Driver's license and registration. Nothing weird here, He did it.

He assumed that the cop was going to run his stuff for any warrants, etc and then explain to him why he was pulled over and anything else that SHOULD be said.

About 5 minutes later he handed him back his license, and registration only and walked away. Jerry said, "Did you give me a ticket or what"? The dullard cop simply nodded his head and said Yes and got in his car and drove away.

AGAIN: Why did officer friendly do this? My first thought was he was one of the many inbred cronies that get hired by their uncles to work there because they got fired at

Wal-mart. In any case did this buy one get one free cop have to say anything? It's a wonder to me also... but...

This is why the police get a bad name. Like the blacks and the "niggers"... this was a COP not an Officer. An officer would have communicated to the person what happened and gave him a chance to explain his action.

Jerry was going 46 in a 30. He did this because the 3 lane highway merged quickly into a 2 lane and he had to get his place in line before he was crowded out and had to wait in a long line.

I know this is the ONE thing that the police can Bully us with, but it's a shame that if Jerry was a minority, he would have most likely at least been talked too. Don't ya think?

CHAPTER 7

LAWYERS, NOT THE TV LAWYERS, THE REAL ONES

My favorite part of any movie or T.V. Show is when this fucking idiot lawyer, pounds in way into the holding cell of his client and pull him out saying, "you don't have anything to hold this guy one, we're leaving".

Do you know what really happens? This fucking lawyer joins his client in the jail cell and they both need to call a real lawyer. Not a Public Pretender...er... defender!

In the real world. The lawyer presents thousands of pounds of paper work and then tells his client that he will try to get him out asap. But, the police can hold him up to 48 (or more per their bought and paid for judge) and the lawyer can do very little indeed, while the police badger the hell outta him until he confesses or just breaks down and bawls.

It more likely goes like this:

Client: But I didn't do it

Cops: Sure you did. Why would you need a lawyer if not

Client: It was the one armed man, I'm telling ya

Later on that next day (or two or three or …)

Cops: This guy did it Sam (the judge)
Judge: Are you sure?
Cops: Sure
Judge: Okay, I'll hold him, so you can get more against him in the court room:
Lawyer: My client has all this proof not to hold him
Judge: Sorry, in my opinion, he will see a grand jury in a month.
Client: What?
Cops: hahaha
Lawyer: But your honor, I disproved everything, and...
Judge: Sorry, counselor, but he will be held (wink to cop).

What pisses me off:
1. The fairy tales of Lawyers, being real people and really caring. The moral vacuum of the law.
2. The constantly accused getting of on technicalities this does not happen at all in any way.
3. The criminals walking free once they're caught. No
4. Juries that really take the time and consider all

Now, what to do:
1. stay the fuck outta trouble
2. stop using race as a weapon
3. EVERYONE inherently knows what is right and wrong. Don't try to say you did not know.
4. Yes, most lawyers suck, so do not get in trouble to find out "law and order" is full of shit.

<u>AESOP:</u> A fox walking by a lion's den was asked by the lion to bring him some food. The Fox replies, "I would, but I see there are many footprints leading into you cave but NONE leading out.

I know a rich man that lives in a mansion, while his girlfriend and daughter live in a trailer park.

Is this right? I don't know. Maybe she is just happy to have a roof over their heads and food on the table. Who knows.

I know a person that has AIDS. He intentionally slept with a gal pal of mine and was nice enough to give her the DEATH Virus. She is dying slowly like him. Should he go to jail? I think so, but hey, who am I? This person will not have a normal life from this day forward.

Chapter 8

Government: Friend or Foe

Unless your governor is Jesse Ventura, the odds are you have another pathological liar, Cut from the Cloth clown or phony front-man for the local band on your hands.

Yes, people there is no "Gene Gatlin" (like on Benson) (what is a "Benson" you are asking. Ah.. fuck off or Google it) that actually takes the time to care about your city hospital, traffic lights or over paid, under worked public employees. The odds are you have a fresh out of college, buy one get one free, pseudo intellectual, glorified teenager actually doing the work on these projects for you.

You know, the ones that sit there in class and just like to argue as a black apologist, fag liberator, or Christian hopeful. "Oh, my dog, how can you even write a book like this...you... you... poopie head!" *Freedom is a TWO EDGED sword for certain.* As you get to defend what you don't like said, I still get to say it. Isn't America super? Yes, I thought so also.

What really pisses me off is:

1. We still are stupid enough to think our votes count
2. We still righteously tell people, "if you do not vote, do not complain". I say, I was an honorably discharged soldier, FUCK YOU, I'll complain all I want to...starting with your dumb ass!
3. Clint Eastwood said it best on MAGNUM FORCE

"The law isn't perfect, but until someone comes along with something better, I am willing to work with it".

Aristotle said, "Happiness begins with us" and this one:

"Democracy arises out of the idea that those who are equal in any respect are equal in all respects; just because all men are equally free, they claim to be absolutely equal".

If I was really smart I would have just quoted Aristotle and my other favorite "A", Aesop and let them use more of the "shoe leather" and I would ride their coattails, but I am so much more colorful.

The government is made by US and only we can change it, ...can just we few, make a difference? Maybe this will help you over the rough spots of life.

Please believe me that this kind of "poetic" shit is best to be left to the dreamers and the unrealistic.

There are no more heroes left in this world, but...

this poem / line, always held so much love and respect for me, I just had to share it with you.

If you still don't like this line / paragraph / etc... Please just watch renaissance man and other *feel good* movies, okay (stupid).

... This story shall the good man teach his son;

And Crispin Crispian shall ne'er go by,
From this day to the ending of the world,
But we in it shall be remembered-
We few, we happy few, we band of brothers;
For he to-day that sheds his blood with me
Shall be my brother; be he ne'er so vile,
This day shall gentle his condition;
And gentlemen in England now-a-bed
Shall think themselves accursed they were not here,
And hold their man-hoods cheap whiles any speaks
That fought with us upon Saint Crispin's day.

I just liked this again, if you did not, write your own fucking book.

CHAPTER 9

SURVIVING TEEN YEARS: BULLYING

Where do you stop and where do you dig in and say, "I shall finish the game" in regards to your whelps. Your children.

WHERE?

Fucked if I know!

No really, there is so much pressure on the world to let their children get away with everything. You know a long time ago, kids got what they deserved. Not toys and candy every trip they made to the stores, but an ASS WACKING every time they threw themselves to the floor because they did not get what they wanted. *Sometimes in this great world, you get what you need, not what you want (yes, I love italics too).*

America does not hand you crap on a silver platter, many times if just offers you hope and the chance to dig in and try. Try a little harder if it's not working at first, but fucking try!

TRY: the most important 3 lettered word in the world. Even more important than mom, dad, god and pay...it's Try.

We have lost the will to tell the government to stay the fuck out of my home, my family, my business, etc.

I own a business where the people I service are much more worried about their items not getting to the ordered place than you life. Is this 'par' for the course or are we so damn dehumanized that everyone has a say in our lives. Everyone?

Here is what pisses me the fuck off:

1. When can your kids just leave? 14, 15, 16, etc...
2. When can they become emancipated teens, get you to pay for everything and now...tah dah... they are in charge! You better have been a monster.
3. When can you do NOTHING but what Dr. Phil, the Government and your nosey neighbors say you can to your children, that you feed and put through the world? When?
4. Should you slap you kids in the mouth for calling you a fucker? Fuck Yeah!!! Many times also!

What I am trying to penetrate in that fucking head of yours is that we have given the government *WAY TO FUCKING MUCH POWER* over us and our kids. By letting the real animals get away with beating and abusing their kids, where we the good people, spank and discipline ours, they are not inter-changeable items and we are never going to win again. We should get a victory once in a while. I will continue to spank my kids into the fucking forties if need be. I am the HNIC period!

Education is the greatest provision to get to an old age:
Thanx again Aristotle, you are so right. Now :

WHO EDUCATES YOUR KIDS in your corner of the world? I sure hope it's you and you were brought up right. I hope!

Poverty is the best parent of Revolution and Crime.
Aristotle
If this is not bad enough, now...you are...

Does this mean you can teach your kids and drink, smoke, do drugs, steal, etc...? No! I means that if you do not make sure your kids are punished, the police will later.

In my days teachers wacked me. If my kid mouths off and the teachers wack her, I will also wack the kid when she gets home for mouthing off a teacher. That is the way it was in my days.

Bullies understand this and act upon it.

My daughter loves to wear crap all over her. She will color her hair, she has piercings (her mom okays it, not me), she has her boyfriend spend the night, etc...

Yes, I want to kill both of them, but my wife thinks we should trust her. I got news for you, she is bullying us.

Kids in school will bully because the teachers, like the cops, are afraid to deal with the real bad kids...BUT, if you are walking the halls to go to the bathroom, you will get detention. Am I the only one that thinks this is fucking stupid and wrong? Probably not, but who will deal with this? Hmmmm?

Chapter 10

Surviving Adult Hood

The most horrible of all growing pains, Growing into your own Adult hood will all it's fancy trimmings and tastes: SUCKS!

Here is your life (yes, Waldo, pretty much everyone's):

- You are born
- You are nurtured (most of us)
- You are put in school; here kids are raised and treated differently, by their parents and possibly their own neighborhood, friends and family
- then you are put into a crock pot of ways to assimilate and grow.
- Some of you start smoking (and yes fuck heads smoking is bad, filthy and not normal, fuck off), drinking, drugs (pot is a drug also, pecker head), bullying, etc... on the flip side
- Some of you are winning trophies, staying in shape, excelling academically, etc.
- Some of you are learning about queer sex education and cop hating too, ... etc

BASICALLY: You were turning into an adult.

In HAMLET, the grave digger says, "on the day you were born, I started digging your grave".

What are our adult feelings? I can only imagine that they change as the years go on: This is your minds progression...

1. 20's: I want to get a good job
2. 30's: I want to get a good wife and family
3. 40's: I want to start thinking retirement
4. 50's: I want to keep doing things I used to
5. 60's: I need to *retire* while there's money
6. 70's: I need to think about a will and *retire*
7. 80's: I need to die soon or *retire*
8. 90's: I need to...holy shit, I lived this long!
9. Over 100: What's your fucking name?
10. Forgot your age: A fucking black president! What's next...a Broad or a Jew? Haha JK.

Welcome to adult hood. There is nothing written in stone for you to grow into: If you were raised isolated, like on a farm and you had a good father: you can be like superman; if you were raised by a bad father: you can be like...

Well Aristotle will tell ya:

> *If some animals are good at hunting and others are more suited to be hunted, then the gods must definitely smile on hunting!*

What kind of animal will you be? I am a bear, big and loveable, but mess with my family: You will die... HORRIBLY!

The government can ruin your life or save it. This is the only *thing* in the world that can do that. Sure your family can help and make sure you're safe, but we pay these people to run around and say, "you're under arrest".

If you think this is an unfair statement.

Pay off your house

Gain your deed

Stop paying taxes

Return to the street. Why, because the government still owns your home and the land you live on...Forever!

This is the reality of your lives. You do not EVER truly own anything. The government we elect (ha ha...Losers) is in total control over us. They will never show you anything that they can hide (from UFO's to the cure for anything).

Even if you do not believe in Aliens, you can believe that our government will hide everything on us. Like any good business, they do not care about you. You are only one small 'nut' in the machine of America.

I love my country.

I hate my government.

Chapter 11

Television Kinda... Sucks!

Television, is there a better social media? I did not think so

Hey, Give me your opinion, right here on this line: *&*(%$#%

That's right: I don't give a shit about your opinions. Remember, *I had to make sure you weren't stupid when you bought this book,* so the last thing I need are you opinions... now, if you are in the ratings system that what you think does not count either. Seriously, did you get the present you wanted for x-mas? Did you get the present you wanted during your religious mass? Keep praying anal cavity, keep praying.

It's almost like a popularity contest as you get together with your friends to see if you watched the popular kids / friends programs: why?

One of my friends used to watch Sanford and Son and picked on my for watching threes company (yes, I am old, fuck you all). I said, "yeah, it's much cooler watching black guys in a junk yard then chicks on a California beach.

When I was in grade school the popular thing to watch was Happy Days, it just came out (again, fuck you, I'm older).

These days:

I will leave what to watch These days alone, because some stupid people may have snuck in to this book and could be reading it right now as we are talking.

I will help you over the rough spots, okay?

What kind of T.V. Do you watch and what does this make you?

What you watch	What you are because of your choice
Vampire Diaries:	Gay or lonely house wife
CNN	Communist
Dr. Phil	Gays and Housewives
Survivor Man	Lonely or a real deprived husbands
the View	VERY FUCKING STUPID
Big Bang Theory	Stop buying comics jerk off
the News (any)	OLD, very fucking OLD
Star Trek / Star Wars	No dates, masturbate constantly
Criminal Minds	Fantasy writers mixed with gay
Blue Bloods	old Magnum P.I. Fan
Sex and the City	Lesbo all the way, LESBIAN
Dexter	Fucking retard, Gay, Imbecilic
SHIELD	not a comic fan, just fucking stupid
Jessica Jones	go and kill yourself
Doctor Who	Gay with overtones of DUMB ASS
Supernatural	STOP MASTURBATING !!!
Grey's Anatomy	is this show still fucking on???
Gotham	with no Batman, probably better

Supergirl	are you fucking kidding me?!?!
NCIS	die Mark Harmon, DIE !
Limitless	Trust me, there's a fucking LIMIT

now...

What you watch	What you most likely are
Black list	probably amount to something
Ash, vs evil dead	not gay, but might be someday
Elementary	good direction. You'll keep your pals
Person of interest	interesting
the Office	I'll hurt you Fairy boy!
Bones	Bone(r)
Jane the Virgin	Do I have to say anything here?
Castle	Best show ever. Fuck off, I love it!
Z-nation	Z = Zero
I Zombie	Jesus Fucking Christ … what?
Walking Dead	Okay, with overtones of If 'ee
Agent Carter	I will shoot your grandmother !
X files	Finally, no one has to die now
NCIS Los Angeles	2 bad actors, 2 bad of a show. 2 bad
unbreakable Kimmy	I hate you
Madam Secretary	start typing bitch
Major Crimes	Never should have got past private
Keeping Kardashians	WHAT the fuck is wrong with you!

The last ship	thank dog, NO Fucking More!
The following	follow fucking what?125# bad actor
Real Rob	I can't bring myself to watch it sorry
NCIS New Orleans	Stop it. Fucking STOP IT!!!!
Crossing Lines	More like, CROSSING EYES
Finding Bigfoot	good show about NOTHING: How do these people stay in Business with no monster? *Oh, I forgot about Congress. If they can keep making themselves look important, I guess an invisible monster can also. Yepper. God damn Fuck Tards!*

People as you can tell, you can stay on T.V. For years and have nothing to offer anyone in the world. Kind of like our Senate

I think T.V. Is like ice cream. Anyone can choose any type of flavor, but when you start choosing Tobacco, Onion and Spit flavored, it is time to thin the fucking herd, okay?

A friend to all is definitely a friend to none. If he/she likes everyone, then he/she has no standards and is too accepting. No one should like or respect a person like this...i.e.; STUPID! You see all these TV show (or movies) where the first five minutes you know the love interests or the best friends to be. I am still fucked up over lethal weapon, I mean really... BFF's. Thank god for PSYCH, or I would never respect weird and opposite people being friends again.

Does TV teach us much? Sure. Good and Bad. Why do they smoke all the fucking time on TV? Because cigarettes cannot be advertised on TV or magazines any more, so movies and tv do it. Is this effective? Hell Yeah.

Don't make me call you an IDIOT again, Okay?

CHAPTER 12

COMPUTER AGE: NEVER LEAVING IT

Yes, the computer will be the death of us all: here is my Formula for this answer:

A = 6
B = 12
C = 18 etc. all the way to Z = 156

Computer spells out = 666
New York spells out = 666

Need I say more? Do I really have too?

No, I am not a fan of the mythic bible, but I do love math and mythology, so any chance to use the mythic mark of the beast, I am fucking in: Not to mention, most of you just had an MI over this little synopsis of mine. Haha. Idiots!

Computer is the easiest way for the government to keep it's loving eyes and arms on you, but...

It's also the easiest way for YOU to keep your eyes and arms on the world and the friends and enemies within.

The computer is the greatest invention since toilet paper and I would not trade it for anything, but are we better off or not with it?

I foresee this for our future:
1. No more snail mail
2. great writers, movie makers and artist
3. super great way to do homework
4. eBay, overstock, AE, finger hut, credit cards, etc.
5. Easiest world ever, but...

I also foresee this for our future:
1. Police can find any little problem and exploit it
2. Bad u tube shows will take over
3. More unique/powerful Viruses all over the world
4. Major Monetary institutions "messed" with
5. Government organizations hacked... hmmmm?

Again, in a nutshell, the good out weighs the bad? I am not sure. Yeah, internet porn is nice, ordering Xmas presents online rocks, but... sometimes easier is not better...

But like firearms, it's not the weapon itself, it's the imbecile using it incorrectly.

I could drone on about this forever (did you get it... drone) but in reality the computer is what it is. It's a way to reach out and meet people, get bills paid on time, talk to family every day, etc...

It is here to stay and will only IMPROVE (?) in time.

Remember again, all myths have a tiny seed of reality to them, I believe.

It is our job as the greatest thinking and dominant life form of Earth to decipher what is real and not.

We have computers and constant links to other people and thinking creatures, overseas that can also add to our ideas (except China...they're all dimwits, dolts and dunderheads and should die) and help us consider all sides of the argument(s).

If you use the computer correctly, it's like any weapon. I can help or hinder your life as good or bad as you use it.

Chapter 13

Why the Amish are So Cool, or Not?

Pound per pound, are the AMISH thinking and living right compared to the world they mostly shun?

I know you are saying, "Ed, what the hell are you talking about these people for? They do not contribute to society or anything"? Yes, they do pay taxes, fix buildings, bake pies, make quilts and other fun things... fuck you if you don't like them. If it makes you feel any better I am sure they do not like you either.

You know what I am going to just make a giant list on this one, we don't even need to separate and hash this one out: HERE:

GOODS	BADS
Not much pollution	Is horseshit pollution
No Cell phone brain deterioration	8th grade education
No Crime	are slow horses a crime

Christianity	Christianity
Home made clothing	again, home made clothing
Craftsmanship	how do you call them to work
Interesting Language	what is that fucking language
no swearing in public or at work	what are they fucking saying
kind words	but, what did they fucking say
Haircuts are real inexpensive	I would pay not to see them
Hats are for sale	Hats are for sale, don't buy!
Always working	how do they have so many kids

Women always working also again, so many fucking kids, how?

Are they German, Dutch, or what? racial discrimination here?

Pleasure in the job, puts perfection in the work.
Aristotle again

I like the Amish, they should be in our standing Army.

I was talking to my friends: One is an Amish, and One is an Alien... ah yes, I did say Alien! Stop running away and saying weirdo, just finish reading the book. It's funny.

Ed: Hi guys, I am glad you could join me for this talk today
Alien: Thank you
Amish: Thank you

Ed: So, who here is enjoying themselves?
Alien: Religion confuses me
Amish: Just believe and all good things come

Ed: Or just work hard and earn them
Alien: Are we still talking about religion?
Amish: Sure that is how you get to heaven. It does not matter
    if you treat animals or non-Amish like crap, just work
    hard.
Ed: We are all confused about religion. The minorities down
    south are as phony as the righteous up here in the north.
    Religion leaves you a door out that says, you can be
    a puke and not burn in a mythic hell as long as at
    your deathbed you ask for forgiveness. I watch people
    stealing, lying, screwing everyone, etc. And these people
    actually believe that this "god" will forgive them at
    death.

They believe because they need too.

Amish: I believe because we are trained at birth too.
Alien: So, if at birth you were told to be and atheist or a devil
    worshiper, you'd be that now?
Ed: so everyone believes differently about the exact same
    book? The bible has produced over 100 types of
    Christianity and all of them have the right idea.

Amish: We don't talk about religion, ever.
Alien: Why do you need religion?
Ed: The same reason you need the government or a bad parent,
    you'd be lost without them. No matter how wrong they are.

The Amish are a unique breed of creature. They basically are shy and mind their own business, but they can be unintentionally imposing and asocial at times. But here's a question; would the world be a better place if we ALL we like them? Think about it before you answer. Think hard!

CHAPTER 14

SOCIAL MEDIA: YOU NEED IT, YOU'RE STILL DUMB

Where do we start here: Face book and Twitter, of course. I do have face book, but not twitter and I have this to say:

1. Friends made on face book and other media sites are grand, but they are not real friends. Unless you consider friends are: not able to be hugged or hand shaken, no Xmas or birthday presents, no real problems; such as: I just got fired again, my wife cheated on me, etc. If you cannot share REAL feelings and trials with them, they're not friends.

2. They don't know you REALLY! No way. I can see you phony fuckers now, "I am a lawyer", "I just got out of the army", "My girlfriend is so hot", "I don't have a wife (as she sits next to you)", etc.

3. as Aristotle would say, "one pretty bird does not make a summer, neither does one pretty day. Likewise, one day or brief time of happiness does not make a person perfectly happy either". You will

never be totally happy with a person adorning you with compliments and the like, if he or she does not really know you. PERIOD. Now grow up!
4. And what pictures or people are real or not?
Social media can be wonderful. It makes the lonely not feel as lonely anymore.
It adds to your life with (pseudo) friends and loves.
It can do much to give you direction.

The people around here make me realize this:
I know this one guy and gal that only want to talk.

They have no intentions of listening to you, they just want to go around and spew out their pseudo intellectual crap and laugh at their own jokes.

...on line: you can opt to dispel these turds, block them, or respond to them *while they are talking or typing to you*, it's fucking great !

It's like promoting the word nigger. Paul Mooney (a black comedian, released a tape called *Race* (according to the New York Times), he says stuff like, "Nigger Vampire", "1-900- blame a nigger", "Niggerstein", "Nigger Raisins" and "Nigger history". Some idiots believe that the word will become less hurtful as it is used more. But, you and I know that is fucking stupid.

If you ever want to get in a fight with a black boy (hey, they call us white boys, so...) just use the word nigger around them.

Remember, RESPECT is a double edged sword. Most of the animals that scream they deserve it, NEVER return it in any way. This word and other actions, simply keep the races separated and confused. No matter what anyone thinks, we are still divided.

CHAPTER 15

JOBS DAMN IT, JOBS!

Oh, I hate my fucking job. It hates me, but... I need it! You are so full of shit.

Yes, you need a job.

Yes, you may not get a better one

Yes, your mother is fucking fat...blah blah blah

I have found a solution to the, "I Hate my job bullshit". Do more than one job you like. Yeah.

Oh, I can hear you lazy fuckers now, "but I have a kid and I can't just..." Fuck you! Keep your legs closed, marry right and have a good life, not a tortured life that you feel as long as you have an excuse for anything, it's okay. Moron!

I work 3 jobs. I hate them all, but I hate them less than one controlling, horrible boss infested job. I am my own boss for all of them and I regret nothing. Yes, it took some money to get started, but only with one of them, the others fell into place shortly after.

Is college necessary? No, but it is helpful.

Now if you:

1. ...*hate life,* don't get a job, kill yourself or go to prison and be taken care of, by everyone!

2. ...*Are spoiled*? Cool, stay at home and live with your parents as long as you can, little problems

3. ...*Win the lottery,* call me mother fuckers, I'll help you spend that money that people say there is no way you can spend in your lifetime. I can!

4. ...*Get the job of your dreams* and you have enough money, a great gal/guy, a nice dog (no cats you fucking freaks, they're just wrong), etc. Congrats! Now shut the fuck up and buy more of my books.

AGAIN: Yes, America can suck, but it can be great also. Again, nothing will be handed to you on a silver plate, just some hope and freedom, and that is all you really need.

Now...

Go get em and stop fucking whining!

You know everything you do in life reflects a thousand times in your life. If you are evil, bad shit WILL happen to you. If you are good, I am sure good things will happen to you. Not because some invisible pal in heaven wills it, but because you worked hard, or you had great support, or you just got lucky. In any case, please, just roll with it. Don't quit. You never know what will happen in this world, so again, expect the worst and hope for the best. Idiot. I had to tell you that. Holy shit!

CHAPTER 16

CHINA FUCKING SUCKS, DEAL WITH IT!

I have been waiting to get to this chapter the entire book !

China is a cesspool full of retards and assholes! Instead of me going on and on, I will fill this chapter with items that I have PERSONALLY experienced, as I had spent 2 horrible years there.

Are you ready for the real China?

Begin:

1. The first thing everyone says is "I'm your friend", Pung yo, is how you say friend in China, that should pretty much some up their relationships.

2. They grope you weirdly, upon meeting you.

3. If you are 10 pounds or more overweight, these disgusting little creatures make mention of it every second of the day. They will tough your belly, and arms, etc. They are assholes

4. they smoke everywhere: at pools, restaurants, etc...

5. They do want to be like Europeans and Americans but as people say, their language and thoughts are way lost in translation.
6. They drink HOT water. Winter, summer, etc... Hot fucking water.
7. Pollution is everywhere. Harbin, had to close down because the pollution reached record numbers in 2015. They are filthy beyond belief.
8. There we 29,000 baby girl fetuses found in the yellow river 6 years ago, so you know they respect their women, and you too.
9. IF they have a female as a first child, they will either; kill it, send it to relatives to raise so they can try for a male, etc. They do this to keep their family scroll going. They are petty and beyond inhuman
10. how they breed dogs are make them fat, put them in a bag and beat them tender, etc. Monsters!
11. I know one couple that had a girl, tried to have it live with their grandparents, got found out and lost all their belongings, as the government came to their house and took everything.
12. It was either winter (-5 degrees) or summer 102 degrees where I lived in the Shandong province. There was no spring or fall, mainly because the horrible pollutions kills their environment.
13. The water must be bought out of plastic canisters, because their water is all polluted. Seriously!
14. They women are degraded so much, that they talk to you with a snicker and slight giggle like they are 6 years old. I guess this turns the males on?
15. All women do there is find a man, marry, have kids

16. They stare at you all day long. Everyday. All the time and they don't care if you see them doing it.

17. They are still communist at heart. If you don't believe me, say, "Mao Se Tung wheres a dress". I said this ONE time in my class and the kids just froze in fear. True story. All of this is, I swear it on my children's lives!

18. They always speak Chinese around you (I mean in the school, not in public). Finally a pal of mine arrived and I speak some Spanish. We had a great time speaking Spanish while those fuckers stared at us and got offended. I lavished every word in Spanish and made sure that they we equally insulted when I said, "yep, now you know how we feel". One stupid male fucker complained to me that they have to help us rent an apartment. NOW, this is how stupid and selfish they really are; he felt we should know there non-Latin based language well enough in 6 months to go out and rent out own apartments; Now this fucking idiot, took 16 years to learn English... do YOU see any massive stupidity here? I do.

19. They treat their boys like Young Emperors. That is their nicknames over here, once you've met them.

20. I can go on forever, but trust me, China is full of dogs and fools, that's why the Japanese hate them.

For the things that we have to LEARN before we can actually do them, we actually learn by doing them.
The Great Aristotle

I know you are saying, "I have been to China and it was great".

Cool,

1. how LONG were you there?
2. Did you bring your children over with you?
3. did you have to sneak out in the middle of the night, to get out of there, or you'd be a prisoner for a long time with your Visa and passport withheld?
4. Did you get to be threatened if you left?
5. did you have to have your agents at the government BRIBED to let you in and stay there?
6. What in all did you do to learn your love of China?

Again, I have sincerely over 100 more horrible times in China I could tell you about, but enough is enough.

DO NOT GO TO CHINA! EVER ! ! !

Chapter 17

Yes Pot, Weed or Marijuana is a Drug, Idiots!

No one loves hearing the retards of the world try to reason out why weed is not a drug. They call it a herb, or just something the man is trying to hide until he can tax it.

Let me tell all you imbeciles one thing: if it is NOT a drug, jerk offs, then let your kids do it.

Stop keeping it to yourselves, give it to junior. Share some cigarettes with them too and let the alcohol flow baby, let it flow.

Instead of harping on this to a bunch of two pack a day smoking, drugged out, alcoholics, let's just think here:

1. All kids should be able to do herbs, or Weed, yes?
2. Let them smoke in schools. Light up and impress all the ugly girls that feel they need to do this to attract the scummy guys, to impregnate them, leave them, and repeat process with other skanks.
3. Alcohol makes every girl prettier at closing time

4. Smoking cigarettes is both smart and alluring: hell yeah, who does not want to lock lips with a ash tray? Fuck yeah, I do... not!
5. Prohibition worked? Nope. Too many two pack a day smoking, pot headed, drunken politicians out there. Clinton will tell ya. Just don't inhale. What?

Aristotle again says:

> What lies in our power to do, also is
> in out power NOT TO DO!

I am not saying that people who do these three evils are evil persons. I am saying they could be even better to themselves and people around them if they did not.

My parents both smoked, my dad drank. They were the best people in the world and I am so happy I was their kid, but

1. Eating at the table with them sucked
2. My dad missed some trips when he drank heavily
3. Every ounce of clothing I word smelled like cigs
4. I remember camping with drunk parents around the campfire, being...well... stupid.

Basically, and I do not care which one of you fucking retards argue with me, there is no reason to drink, smoke or do drugs.

Grow up and take responsibility for your own lives

CHAPTER 18

STUPID MOVIES OF ALL TIMES

Now how do you gauge a stupid movie? Everyone has their own taste and support their own favorite actors.

Here is how you do it...

BECAUSE they fucking SUCK SHIT!

Here are some prime examples:

1. Twilight and anything associated with it
2. Batman, new and old. He needs to learn to kill. It is fun and practical for a dude with NO POWERS.
3. 50 shades of Grey. No matter the shade.
4. Anything with a "Rapper" in it, they suck too!
5. Basically, Anything my wife watches sucks.
6. Anything that does not use special effects
7. People think if it hits home it's great. I say the opposite, if it hits home, why watch it, you live it! At the end of any labor is the treat to gain Leisure. Aristotle again summed it up nicely. ...Why work your ass off

to gain some time off
to watch a jerk off?
If you do than fuck off?
    Nothing more needed here.

CHAPTER 19

IF YOU COULD READ MINDS...?

Here is the acid test to self discovery...
You don't need fucking Jesus
You don't need fucking College
You don't need mommy and daddy. (Well?)

If you can have someone read your mind and still be your friend, then you have a real friend.

What do you think would happen if you could read:

1. Your Wife's mind
2. Your Dog's mind (yes, I am serious)
3. Your Parent's mind
4. Your Friend's mind
5. Your Boss's mind
6. Your Banker's mind
7. a Stranger's mind
8. a Priest's mind (haha)
9. a psychiatrist's mind
10. and finally, a kids mind.

All these can come to a head and tell you your real soul. This type of power would be lethal, and we have it. Truth serum or other types of stimulants. What would happen after wards.

Let's start with your Wife's mind. What could be a worst test subject buy the gal you are planning on spending your life with, just to find out...well...you suck!

- She thinks your wee wee is too small
- she has a boyfriend
- she thinks your kids are not yours
- she nailed your friend, brother, father, etc.
- she has AIDS
- she has to satisfy herself after you're done
- she is a sleeper agent and your being watched, etc.

I mean can there be much else to top this?

You're probably saying, "why the hell is he asking this and what would he care what a dog thinks"?

Well I think I am like everyone else in the world. I would like to be rich, perfect, immortal, powerful, etc. I doubt there is anyone that dreams of mediocrity. If there is, email me immediately and I will have you wacked, dragged from your house and pounded by a rhino. You're a waste of space.

The end all see all again is, what are you living for?

Youth is easy to lie too, because it is so quick to hope for truth!

Aristotle again sums up the world in a sentence. *We can all be lied to, but sooner or later we will see the only real hope is the one that WE instill in OURSELVES.*

I am the greatest person in the world...because I said so.

I only need to wrap my loving arms around myself and be happy.

Most of you are saying, "what a tool" and crap like that. That is fine. Be honest. I mean I know you're NOT honest with:

1.   your coworkers
2.   your spiritual leader
3.   your husbands or wives
4.   your boss
5.   most of your friends
6.   your kids for sure (Liars)!
7.   Your old school pals
8.   your Fb, or other media pals, etc...

So at least be honest with me. I can take it. Why:

Because I lion does not care what a sheep thinks!

CHAPTER 20

MY ALIEN FRIEND AND I HAVE HAD SOME GREAT CONVERSATIONS

My alien buddy and I have talked in great detail. Here is / are some of our discussions. Yes, I am generous and I thought you would like to hear what we have discussed. He calls me Eddi and I call him "A". (he likes it). (yes we are going to have more conversations like this. I enjoy them. so... yadadaa... go and suck it. It's my book and i'm entertaining your dumb ass.

A: Eddi, tell me about your country

Eddi: Well, it's a vast land that has great control over the world

A: How does it do that?

Eddi: with diplomacy and money

A: so if your country was as small as say, Luxemburg, could they control and offer as much to the world?

Eddi: No, of course not.

A: so they are only as popular as they are safe from invasion, running out of money, and have great technology?

Eddi: Yep, that about sums it up

A: Eddi, what is homosexuality?

Eddi: It is the act of two people of the same sex, having sex

A: Why do they do this?

Eddi: I think it's because they are attracted to the same sex

A: Are you this way

Eddi: No, I am proud to say, I love women

A: What makes them love the same sex

Eddi: Mostly Abuse or neglect of some kind, but some of these people believe you are born this way?

A: So if you are a certain Political or Religious type are you born that way also

Eddi: I certainly hope not, I am certain, no one is born a certain way. We are in a land of freedom and 99% of our choices are ours

A: So, can they be born liking a certain food as this seems more of a similar choice

Eddi: I think this is a good idea, as you are brought up eating a certain food, it is much more likely.

A: So when homos are born this way, they never have a girl friend or kiss a girl. Does it disgust them?

Eddi: I am not sure. I know some do, but others...not sure. I often wondered about this myself. When did it start? It's kinda like asking a girl when she lost her viginity, some actually don't know or have blocked it out.

A: Eddi, What is discrimination?

Eddi: This is when someone is not liked as much or does not get treated the same as others.

A: What types of people are these?

Eddi: Well, there are the Blacks who were most recently slaves..

A: A slave is someone who is forced to do things for a master

Eddi: Yes

A: So are you a slave also, Eddi?

Eddi: Hmmm. Yes, I am. I am a slave to a public that may or may not support my business.

A: But can't you just leave your business?

Eddi: Yes and No. I can, but I will be very poor and have to work for other people, whom care mostly for the dollar not the person working.

A: So are free with conditions

Eddi: Yes

A: So when you discriminate you take away freedom?

Eddi: Yes and No. You take away some of their freedom to work and earn money to support their families, but they can go some where else to find work. Like an ex-prisoner is discriminated too.

A: So why were there slaves? Who made them slaves?

Eddi: Mostly their own people sold them into slavery, but it's kinda like drugs...if there are no demands then the bad guys don't get any sales.

A: I think I understand

A: Eddi, here is the big question I have, "What is Religion"?

Eddi: Ah, this one has plagued man for years, are you ready?

A: Yes

Eddi: Man needed to control people in the early stages or ages in our development. So we created gods. These gods were mostly men and designed to keep people, women and enemies in their respective places, while earning a place in history and society.

A: You mean keep them away

Eddi: Yes, or at a comfortable arms distance

A: I think I see, go on please.

Eddi: One of the final acts of creating gods was to make one giant god above all others. This started with ODIN the All Father in Norse mythology. This religion dominated for many years, as our days of the weeks we named after them. Tuesday is Tyrs day, the god of war. Wednesday is Odin or Woden's day, the middle of the week. Thursday was named after Thor and Friday after Frigga or Freya the mother of Thor wife of Odin.

A: This is kinda exciting

Eddi: You haven't hit gold yet. Finally as the world formed, we needed a better or easier book that would convince us that all religion was formed from one type of god. It's called Christianity

A: This came about how?

Eddi: Oh, the children of the world are very easily duped and led astray. A man named Constantine (a Caesar) allowed the first type of Christianity to come about on his death bed. He saw how these people would die for this myth and he thought it would be a great income and control tactic for his Roman's, ergo, Christianity was born and the myth spread.

A: When does or did this god originally show himself?

Eddi: Oh, man, A, you are going to love this one. He never has.

A: What do you mean, there must be some proof and constant on going proof of his or her existence?

Eddi: Nope, people say he was born from himself

A: What?

Eddi: Yeah, he sent his only begotten son, which was indeed himself, and sacrificed himself, and...

A: What are you talking about? I asked when he proved himself and granted wishes, etc.

Eddi: Well, he really never has and never will. These people believe that he is to be respected and revered just on faith.

A: What kind of idiots pray and tithe...

Eddi: 10 – 20% of their income at that

A: ...to a non-existent being?

Eddi: We are desperate for a savior to unite the world and save and love each other. Since there is not one around that can walk the Earth or even be proven to exist, these people live on hopes.

A: So, what is the difference of a fake god or one that does not show or prove his existence?

Eddi: We are afraid of death

A: Where do these Christians go when they die?

Eddi: To a perfect utopia or a heaven where they are reunited …

A: Why do they cry when their loved ones die?

Eddi: I guess they are uncertain of where they are going, because there is another spot in the after life where they stir coals and are suffering for all eternity

A: What? What kind of good god would allow this?

Eddi: He not only allow this, he condones this. He created this.

A: What?

Edward J. Rydzy

Eddi: He created all the angels and Satan, the Ruler of hell is a fallen angel that is allowed to bring them to hell and torture them

A: What!

Eddi: Well, only the disbelievers that don't tithe to him, and such

A: So. What if you are in a place that has never heard of him?

Eddi: Then I guess you go to Limbo?

A: So, why don't these people go and spread the word?

Eddi: I sincerely don't know.

A: Let me get this straight now, because this in on your dollar bill in your land of freedom

Eddi: Yep

A: You have a god that your country has on it's currency

Eddi: Yep

A: This god does not ever walk among you and prove himself

Eddi: Yep

A: You tithe to him

Eddi: Well, yep, but some people claim he talks to them.

A: Are they better people for it?

Eddi: Some priests do bad things

A: I do not get this.

Eddi: I handed him a bible and 'A' looked at it and read it quickly

A: This is the word of a god

Eddi: Some say "the" god

A: This book constantly contradicts itself

Eddi: And, the chapters in it were allowed by a group of elders

A: How can only certain chapters of a great god be allowed in

Eddi: Men created this book and god in their own image

A: This is why the women are told to be quiet and such.

Eddi: I can only imagine, but this is not why I gave you this book to read.

A: You're kidding me, there is more.

Eddi: There are wars that are still going on over this book.

A: People are killing people over this book.

Eddi: Yes, but the reason I had you read this entire book, is because most priest and teachers of this book do NOT read it all.

A: Why not

Eddi: in the "olde days" the book was in Latin and only the few higher educated persons could read it at all. To this day, there is no real education or readings of it in great details. I would challenge any church or teaching group to read and actually study the entire book, front to back, acknowledging the contradictions and still believing this was the word of a great good and not just a bigoted bunch of old fools trying to get control of the simple.

A: Eddi, I have changed my mind, I will visit you another time when your world has grown up and doesn't want to kill for land and out dated beliefs.

Eddi: So, I will never meet you face to face?

A: Just like your god, you'll have to have faith you did. The Amish and I have told you enough. You'll learn the truth...

Eddi: The Amish! Damn it! I knew it. They are not from this world... where? Jersey? Ireland? Tell meeeeeeee........

CHAPTER 21

THE SUPERNATURAL VERSUS REALITY

Now, what scares me here is that I have to actually make up a chapter on this.

For all you bright eyed idiots that believe in the supernatural but not this god crap, please come to a book signing so I can hit you in the face with this book...multiple times. Ass!

Let's hit the big 4:

- God
- Bigfoot
- Ghosts
- and UFO's

I have beat up the myth of god enough, so lets move on. Bigfoot:

Okay, I know there are dullards out there whom like Bobo, Cliff, Ranae and Matt...Please go FUCK yourselves. Please.

They have not fucking found anything but an insanity plea. I have seen more believable mediums talking to a crystal ball on the fucking table then: "A pile of leaves, it's a squatch"... "foot prints, had to be a squatch"... "I can't tell what this picture is off, ... squatch". WHAT??? Where did your I.Q.s go?

If I was to tell anyone this, I'd be in a New Jersey *hot house* and I don't mean sauna.

There is no proof of any kind that there is a bigfoot. Now, is it possible that there could be? Sure. There is also possibility that there is a lochness monster...or even a yeti, or...whatever. But, the punchline to this endless joke is, PROVE IT!

How many courts of law accept this line of shit? It's like why do we not get taught religion in schools? Because Mythology is a college level, semi-debatable topic/subject. It's not for the meek or young to hash out. It for the pseudo intellectual students to test their weak ass'd, disrespectful new mind muscles on, because we (in the real world) don't fucking care. We're too busy trying to pay for their fucking loans.

Enough of this furry fuck, how about Ghosts?

Yeah, I often find myself in the corner of a dark room just hoping that Hitlers ghost will come and try to rape my cat or something stupid like that.

But let me thank pudding heads like Ghost Adventures, Ghost Hunters, Ghost Brothers, Ghost... fuckers...

Come on people. Jesus fucking Christ...REALLY! Why do they always hunt at night or in the dark? Are ghosts afraid of the light? No! They do it because there are all sorts of light anomalies that can affect a camera, at NIGHT! Idiots.

"Well Ed, I have actually seen a ghost and..." Please, fucking die; become one; and come back and scream in my face like a banshee and say, "You see, mother fucker. I told you there were ghost". Then, I will believe you.

I always said to myself, if my mother could come back and scold me for how I spent my inheritance, she fucking would have by now and my life would have made hell look like full fucking house.

Now UFOs are a sticking situation. I mean this is the iching of what not to report. The reason being, all you can say is "I seen it but it flew away before I could get a picture". Tah dah. You're on Geraldo explaining yourself. Maury apologizing and Dr. Phil, crying.

If I just spent 400 light years traveling through the fucking gigantic galaxy, I would not just "hit and run" the first sign of (semi) intelligence I ran into.

Here is what I would do;
1. I would stop.
2. I would make out with a hot earth beotch
3. I would bang a hot earth beotch
4. I would bring back currency
5. I would bring back precious gems
6. I would bring back people
7. I would write a martian book on my earth trip
8. I would eat all types of earth food
9. I would talk to their LEADER
10. I would exchange mechanical crap, etc...

Do you see where I am going with that. Not just pop in and get scared away by, what we would consider, Noahs ark versus the fucking Starship Enterprise.

Let's all put our minds together here and reminisce about what uncle Ed has fucking drilled into your scant gray matter.

No Bigfoot. Nothing. No bones. No good pictures, and don't even mention that stupid Patterson / Gimlin film. Patterson was a con man and the entire film was shit. I could do better.

Ghosts: I think anyone who BELIEVES they saw a ghost was most likely a terrified delusion at best, a complete break down at worst. If there were ghost, IDIOTS, they'd stick around and talk to their families. They'd want to be seen to make their families famous and have a great life. They'd want to be seen to try to get their life back OR to tell everyone that the afterlife is real and good. So, fuck off.

UFO's... NO. Use logic, stop being stupid or I'll tell the government to send out more of their fake planes to mess with you.

I am sorry people, I wish there was a benevolent god, cool furry fucking ape stalking the world, Casper the friendly ghosts and some cool UFOs to give me a kicking ride to Austrailia to meet some hot beach babes...but there is not.

Be a thinking creature, the government is counting on you being the imbeciles you always have been. Grow the fuck up. I cannot go state to state, country to country and wet nurse your neurosis.

Grow up and think for yourselves or there are many people that will be happy to do your thinking for you. Trust me.

Which is a great lead in for the next chapter.

Chapter 22

Shit sucking college and school students from hell.

Hey, you raised them.

I want to see these courses taught in college for these fucking bright eyed idiots:

1. Does Bigfoot suck (in any way)
2. Why do you constantly walk in front of cars, ASS! Crosswalks are not optional. How about a sense of Urgency please. Li
3. Gay, Lesbian, and Trannie Shit, for Dummies
4. Why being an argumentative bitch will not get you a lawyers job, it will get you this: "Hi, welcome to McDonalds, may I take your order"? Well, at $15 an hour, I may skip college completely...etc...

I drive by a college 4 days a week. And, every time I pass it there are some *galactically* stupid, anti-intellectual, stupid, selfish, mean, young fucking "I think I know it all", god damn kids just walking at the speed of farm, right across the crosswalks and texting. They look at you as if to say, "you can't run over me, or all the world will come to my aid and sue you".

If that's not bad enough, now they got these uber stupid fucking children (from 6 – 12) doing the exact same fucking thing. They also just stare at you.

People, your coddling of these kids (all ages) is not teaching them any respect for the dangers of the roads at all. As far as I am concerned, college "kids" can go fuck themselves. If they get in my way, they should be immediately put to death any way.

I mean that just shows me:

1. no respect
2. no sense of urgency to keep the flow of traffic flowing
3. a total disregard for the real world.

One kid jumped back out on to the road, for god knows what fucking reason and wanted to stand off against me while I was driving at him. I was not of course, but I guess he was put out that I did not have to stop or slow down, because he already made it across the street.

College does not teach common sense or respect.
Period!
I think all these fucks should have to do a few things:
- Get drug tested monthly
- Learn customs and courtesies as a minor, for life

- let them work in the real world and with a real man
- let them have REAL people come in and lecture them, not some burnt out author (haha), with his degrees flying like banners as they walk in.

College does nothing for you without class...and class and money are so different. If you don't know that, then please DIE !

I have to insert this last little bit, Okay?

College will not teach you...:

1. common sense
2. respect
3. worldly traits
4. common courtesies
5. stay alert, stay alive mentality
6. to love your fellow man
7. genuine work ethics... show up on time, etc

Another fun side note. I know these two people, one is a business man and the other a teacher. They buy the weed by the pound. They are serving your community and teaching your kids real good values, I am betting.

Titles are simply titles. Just because they have not spent a night in jail, it does not mean they should not.

CHAPTER 23

WOMEN

How could you entitle a chapter of your book with such a sexist remark. Hey, if Johnny Cockrum can do it to Marsha, then damn it, so can I.

I am not going to flatten women out and call them a bunch of names, even though it would be fun, I still like them very, very much. I enjoy them physically, but ... mentally... we have to talk.

Now I know you females go from one end of the spectrum to the other.

Sometimes you're the ultra geniuses and we're the idiots.

Sometimes you're the domestically abused airheads.

But in all the cases we keep you around for what's between your legs...and I'm not talking about those droopy-assed belts, strangle me 'daisy dukes' or the tramp stamps that just compliment a psycho bitch so much.

Here is my main complaint:

Do you want a nice guy? Of course not. I know this and so do the massive amounts of unmarried men that look like mutants and not the cool ones like on the X-men (yay Marvel Universe).

You cannot have doors opened for you and want to be a 21st century woman too. Sorry, Nazi-bitch, Choose! Just read this book and be a real person. Okay?

Chapter 24

Racial Retardation

Okay the most sensitive issue on our planet... NO!

I see a lot of stupid things said and done on this Earth, but the word Nigger is the most stupid of them all.

Do you think Martin Luther King would admire this idiotic word 'spewed' all over their Rap records?

Did common sense just drop off the planet.

Hey, and then there is the "avengers" of the word, whom will turn into mentally retarded children if they hear it and scream or try to kill you. Nothing stupid there...NOT!

Do I go up to Polish people and say "yo! My Pollock, what up, stupid ass"? No, because it's asinine.

If you buy an album with the words NIGGER, BITCH, HO, WHITE BOY, etc... on it, you deserve what you're going to get in life. A look of "OMG, you're a fucktard"!

Bill Mayer uses the term (as others do) Morally Bankrupt. This is an adventurous term that simply means..."The state of being devoid of morality and ethics, used esp. for business and political entities". Ethics: "moral principles that govern a person's or groups behavior" or "a branch of

KNOWLEDGE that deals with moral principles". Haha Are you fucking kidding me?

Where the hell do you find this "Branch" these days?

What possible Tree does it grow on? Yggdrasil in Asgard?

If this is the tree you are talking about that sheds those beautiful branches, you fucks better be ready to sacrifice an eye to get it... and I fucking know you're not going to do that. Most of you won't sacrifice the body of Christ in a mass for it.

Do you know the word SHIT came from the abbreviations for Ship High In Transit, for the methane build up in old crafts of yesteryear... where did the world Nigger come from? Niger? Who fucking cares.

Do you rapping retards understand that there are probably thousands of skin heads just laughing there asses off every time you use this word.

When you are in pain or degraded, the people that hate you ... WIN ! ! !

It's kinda like the people that drink, smoke and do drugs. I (again) do NOT want them to stop. Most of these fucks I love seeing die slowly and killing the people and animals closest to them. It fucking rocks.

If you're too weak or ignorant to stop, go baby, go! Don't let me stop you.

This wisdom (riiiight) applies to the people that use the word nigger. Hell yeah. It does not hurt my feelings, but it does hurt black peoples (or people of color, colored people, African American, or...whatever the fuck they call themselves these days) feelings or they would not react hostile to it.

Nigger: a contemptuous team for a black or dark skinned person.

These is no justification for this world.

It is a domination attempt of the black people to use the word and others not allowed to use it. It's retarded, right Martin?

Now, I know there are MANY blacks (or or people of color, colored people, African American, or...whatever the fuck they call themselves these days) that are absolutely disgusted by this word and to those persons, I sincerely salute you... but, stop buying the fucking albums. It's like voting for a president, STOP. You're just encouraging the fucks to keep running, okay?

Everyone of you (above sixteen or so) know what is right and wrong. Again, the fact that I have to write this is beyond me.

I know women whom get beaten by men and men that get beaten on by women. Both know this treatment is horribly wrong but again, what will become of this? Will it get worse or better?

The ironic thing is at this point in time, words like this keep bigotry alive. But remember people, it's the people that keep it alive, not the words.

CHAPTER 25

THE FRIENDS I'VE KNOWN

I could not in good conscious leave this book as it is without talking to you about the friends i've known.

Friend ONE: **BEFORE**: He cheated at everything he ever did. Was the worst kid I could have imagined.

NOW: He teaches I.T. At a school

Friend TWO: **BEFORE**: He got his wife pregnant at 16, he had to run to Georgia to get married to avoid prosecution. He hit his mother with *nunchucks* and lied about any degree he said he had obtained or has since gotten.

NOW: He works for a major insurance company and tries to be a righteous member of the community

Friend THREE: **BEFORE:** He did drugs so much his nickname was drugs

      NOW: He works as a QC person in a major production company.

Friend FOUR: **BEFORE:** this one spent all his time complaining about COKE Highes (coca cola), claimed he had untra-sonic hearing, etc...

      NOW: He is in the Air Force. Nice play

Friend FIVE: **BEFORE:** Dated and slept with I do not know how many guys.

      NOW: Works for the government handing out loans and college approvals, or something like that.

Friend SIX: **BEFORE:** This kid would kick people legs out from under them and laugh.

      NOW: He is the chief of Police

There are many others. Do I write this saying, people never change and even has adolescence they must get what they deserve out of life. Every pie in the face, every water balloon, every stupid things we did has youth's should haunt us forever?

NO WAY.

But what I am saying it...
Your past does not define you
Your Sexuality does not define you
Your Origin/Race does not define you
Nothing defines you but YOU. You can be anything you want to be. You can change; VINCE LOMBARDI said,

"Winning in not a sometimes thing, it's an all the times thing, but unfortunately, so is Losing".

AGAIN: Every god damn person knows what is right and wrong. Now get out there and fucking do it.

...

DO
NOT
MAKE
ME
WRITE
A
SEQUAL

EPILOGUE

I have droned on for many hours trying to explain to you why I have such a hate, dislike or disappointment in humanity. I don't do it because I was brought up mean and unloved. I do it because I was brought up loved, in a well to do family and wish the world was the same.

I wish the world never changed. In my days kids could go to the pool down the street and not worry about being picked up, stolen or introduced to drugs or horrible music. We kept to ourselves and enjoyed family time.

We were not ridiculed for unpopular shirts, shoes or music.

The world did not hate cops/police or lawyers. We worked with them and respected them. It was not a get over to make money, there were laws and rules. Lawyers only took care of deeds to lands, major mergers and the (VERY) Occasional honest accidents people had.

Teachers were revered and loved. They were allowed to dole out a certain amount of punishment and gain respect from the students and parents.

Parents were the sole or greatest contributor to their child's upbringing and well-being, not Madonna or some scum bag rapper, but the parents.

You all goddamn know what's right and wrong. Shame on you all.

OKAY:

now that you've read the entire book, here are my BIBLE contradictions or stupid comments that I promised you:

FIRST: buy the book, "Deceptions and myths of the bible, By Lawrence Graham. I know I should not promote another persons book, but this guys a genius.

SECOND: go online and look up Bible Contradictions

THIRD: use my email and talk to me.

The trick to life is to always question and learn.

Never stop growing. It's just like a business.

Grow or Go!

You are still probably confused as to why I wrote this book. Well... here is a questionnaire to help you over the rough spots in life: fill it out or I WILL hunt you down... and do horrible things to your cat.

How to know if you were too stupid to have bought this book:

1. Do you believe in god just because of the   Y N
   bible?

2. Do you think Police are evil bastards?   Y N

3. Do you believe in Bigfoot?   Y N

4. Do you think the Chinese will rule the world?   Y N

5. Is there no one on the road when you are driving?   Y N

6. Do you like Cats better than Dogs?   Y N

7. Do people wait for you while you buy lottery?   Y N

8. Does your child have the right to boss you around?   Y N

9. Do you vote?   Y N

10. Do you use the word nigger and are indeed black?   Y N

11. Are you gay and tell every fucking person?   Y N

12. Are you a retard, but not in fact retarded?   Y N

13. Do you love to text or talk on your phone in a car?   Y N

14. Are you a teenager?   Y N

15. Do you think POT is not a drug?   Y N

16. Do you think Batman can really beat Superman?   Y N

17. Did you watch Twilight?   Y N

18. Did you watch all the Twilight saga shit movies?   Y N

19. Did you think Edward was cute in any way?   Y N

20. Will you watch twilight again, ever?   <u>Y N</u>

21. If you watch twilight again, will you kill yourself?   Y N

22. If you don't believe in suicide will a friend
    kill you?Y N
23. Will you at least drink poison if you love   Y N
    Edward?
24. Will you throw this book away if you   Y N
    have a poster of Edward anywhere in your
    room, car, or anywhere?
25. Will you promise to punch anyone in the   Y N
    face that says, if you don't vote, you can't
    complain?
26. Will you promise to say bloody Mary in   Y N
    the mirror, and then say, Jesus Christ also
    and see what happens?
27. Will you go into a restaurant and order   Y N
    a glass of water, a tuna-fish pie, and 75
    napkins and see what happens?
28. Will you promise to call those Apes on   Y N
    "finding Bigfoot and say you've mated
    with a Yeti?
29. Will you masturbate to an Xfiles character Y N
    tonight?
30. Will you kiss an Amish person?   Y N
31. Will you watch TV every day and   Y N
    enjoy it?
32. Will you get a shitty job that pays well?   Y N
33. Will you go to church in your underwear   Y N
    just once?
34. Will you wear a mask to McDonalds   Y N
    and just sit there and stare at all the
    employees, just once?

35. Will you promise to try to read peoples minds? Y N

36. Will you say, "China Sucks" once every day? Y N

37. Will you tell your mother you've seen a ghost? Every day? Even if you're not living at home? And you're gay? Y N

38. Will you promise to try to learn common sense in college along with the Periodic Table and shit? Y N

39. Will you stop DRIVING IN FRONT OF ME? Y N

40. Will you buy this book and learn something from it? <u>Y N</u>

The first 20 (1 - 20) should be all: No
The next 20 (21 – 40) should be all: Yes {2 points a question?}
Here's the 10 pt bonus question: Did this book offend you? Y **N**

CREDITS:

Cathy Luffman: Thank you for my wraparound cover. Great shot

Diane Rydzy (my wife): for working two jobs to allow me to keep writing this book and trying to give us a better life. Or maybe at least a pool someday.

Fox and Raven Rydzy (my kids): for giving me the courage to write this fourth book, with my fingers crossed.

FAVORITE QUOTES that I've found on the internet. Thank you

1. A lion does not lose sleep over the opinions of a sheep.
2. It takes a special person to risk so much for people that care so damn little (police quote).
3. Being able to respond instantly with Sarcasm is actually a sign of a healthy brain (so go fuck yourselves).
4. You post all your personal shit on "social media" and you get offended when people judge you? You're a special kind of stupid aren't you?
5. You're tired of my ANTI-Religious post... why don't you just pray for me to stop.
6. Do you know what the difference between the prime directive and your mother is? I have never violated the prime directive.
7. A better bible, 4 words: Don't be a dick!
8. I am not judging you for doing something... I am judging you for putting it, loud and proud, on social media. Idiots!
9. Christianity: the belief that somne cosmic Jewish Zomie can make you live forever if you symbolically eat his flesh and telepathically tell him that you accept him as your master, so he can remove an evil force from your soul that is present in humanity because, a rib-woman was convinced by a talking snake to eat from a magical tree, that held the wisdom of the knowledge of right and wrong
10. fuck off and make real friends in the real world!

11. Recession is when your neighbor loses his job. Depression is when you lose your job. And Recovery is when the President loses his fucking job.
12. Please tell me your problems, I need a laugh.
13. A large group of Baboons is called a Congress. Yep
14. Jesus spelled backwards sounds like Sausage
15. Fuck math... i'll be a stripper
16. I love everyone. Some I love to e around, some I love to avoid, and others i'd love to punch in the fucking face.
17. If you feel like shit, everyone you hate wins!
18. Everything happens for a reason...but, sometimes the reason is you're fucking stupid and make bad decisions.
19. If you repeat a lie enough, it becomes POLITICS

Life is not fair, get used to it and fuck off
The world doesn't care about you, unless you accomplish something
You won't make 60k a year outta school, you actually must earn it first
If you think your teacher is tough, wait until you get a … BOSS
Flipping burgers is an opportunity, not a degradation
Learn from your parents/teachers mistakes. Don't blame them if U don't learn
Parents are boring from: paying bills, worrying about you, cleaning, etc...
Schools doing away with losers, holding kids back, etc. Needed, but not real.
Employers don't give you time to find yourself, learn that on your own time

> TV us not real life. Real life, people leave the coffee shop and go to work.

> Be nice to nerds, the chances are they will become your bosses in the future

20. America: designed by geniuses and run by Idiots

21. Tell people there's an invisible man in the sky who created the universe, and the vast majority will believe you. Tell them the paint is wet and they'll have to fucking touch it!

22. My father was killed by Ninja's, need $ for karate lessons

23. I don't want to be wrong so the wrong people can be right

24. Jimmy Carter said, "if you fear making anyone mad, then you ultimately probe for the lowest common denominator of human achievement.

25. Last thing, some religious oddities for you to think about:

2000 years ago: Jesus   5000 years ago: Horus

Born of a virgin	Born of a virgin
Birthday on December 25th	Birthday on December 25th
North star led men to him when he was born	North star led men to him when he was born
Taken to Egypt to escape the wrath of Herod	Taken to Egypt to escape the wrath of Typhon
Taught in the temple as a child	Taught in the temple as a child
Baptized by John the baptist and had 12 disciples	Baptized by Anup the baptist and had 12 disciples

Performed miracles	Performed miracles
Walked on water	Walked on water
Was transformed on a mountain	Was transformed on a mountain
Titles included: the way, the light, the truth, the messiah, God's anointed son, son of man, the good shepherd, lamb of God, the word, the morning star, the light of the world	Titles included: the way, the light, the truth, the messiah, God's anointed son, son of man, the good shepherd, lamb of God, the word, the morning star, the light of the world
Crucified. Buried in a tomb and resurrected.	Crucified. Buried in a tomb and resurrected.

I sincerely hope you've grown from this book... in this world, you either get BETTER or BITTER.

About the Author

Ed has been there and done that. He has an honorable discharge from the army, went to college, hiked Europe, and taught in China. He has lived in many different states and been to college four times. He has seen a lot and is now sharing his views, wisdom, and adventures in this brutally honest, thought-stirring book written with harsh language. Do not read this if you are faint of heart. It is adult material—for adults only.

Printed in the United States
By Bookmasters